Puppies and Kittens

By Fran Manushkin

Illustrated by Ruth Sanderson

A GOLDEN BOOK • NEW YORK

Golden Books Publishing Company, Inc., Racine, Wisconsin 53404

Everybody loves puppies and kittens! They are so much fun to watch and to hold and to play with. There are so many fascinating things to know about them, too!

Puppies and kittens are born with their eyes closed. For about the first ten days of their lives they cannot see at all. They find their mother by smelling and touching her.

After about two weeks puppies and kittens can open their eyes and see the world around them.

While they are small and helpless, kittens and puppies must stay close to their mothers, who watch over them and give them milk to drink.

As puppies and kittens grow bigger they learn to play with their brothers and sisters. They have a wonderful time running and leaping and even pouncing on each other!

All of these skills will be very useful to them when they grow up and need to defend themselves.

Puppies and kittens use their noses to sniff out food and to recognize friends. If you are eating something delicious, a kitten or a puppy will smell it and come running!

A kitten can curl its tongue into a spoon shape for drinking milk. A kitten will also use its rough tongue to lick itself clean after a meal.

As puppies grow, their teeth get bigger and sharper so they can eat meat more easily.

Have you ever noticed how puppies and kittens can move their ears in ways that people can't? Kittens can turn their ears to discover exactly where a sound is coming from. Even when kittens are sleeping, they keep their ears straight up, ready to catch the slightest sound!

Puppies tilt their heads to help them hear
sounds that are coming from in front of them.

You can usually guess what kind of mood a kitten is in by looking at its tail. A happy kitten holds its tail up proudly. But an angry kitten will lower its tail.

Kittens also use their tails to help keep their balance when they walk through narrow spaces.

You can always tell when puppies are happy,
because they wag their tails wildly.

All kittens and puppies have soft furry paws. But kittens have sharp claws inside their paws. These claws will help them to defend themselves and catch mice.

Kittens often sharpen their claws on the rough bark of a tree. Sometimes a kitten will climb high up in a tree and have trouble getting back down!

Kittens can be all different colors. They can be orange, black, white, gray, tan, or brown, or even more than one color.

Some kittens, such as the Angora and the Persian, have long silky fur. Others, such as the Siamese and the American Shorthair, have shorter fur. No matter whether it is short or long, a kitten's fur is very important. The fur protects the kitten and keeps it warm.

Puppies can be many colors and sizes. Some small puppies can grow up to be almost as big as a little pony. Other dogs are so small, you can hold them in the palm of your hand. The smallest dog is the Chihuahua. One of the biggest is the Great Dane.

There is something very special about puppies and kittens. It's fun to watch them as they play and as they grow up to be adult dogs and cats. If puppies and kittens are treated with care and love, they will grow up to be wonderful pets and good friends, too.